P9-DWG-827

D0037601

ONE MONDAY MORNING

By Uri Shulevitz

Charles Scribner's Sons / New York

An elaboration of the ancient French folk song "Lundi matin, l'emp'reur,
sa femme…" / Copyright © 1967 Uri Shulevitz / This book published
simultaneously in the United States of America and in Canada — Copyright under the Berne Convention / All rights reserved / No part of
this book may be reproduced in any form without the permission of
Charles Scribner's Sons
Printed in the United States of America

Library of Congress Catalog Card Number 66-24483
ISBN: 0-684-13195-1 (cloth)
ISBN: 684-16009-9 (paper)

7 9 11 13 15 17 19 RD/C 20 18 16 14 12 10 8
1 3 5 7 9 11 13 15 17 19 RD/P 20 18 16 14 12 10 8 6 4 2

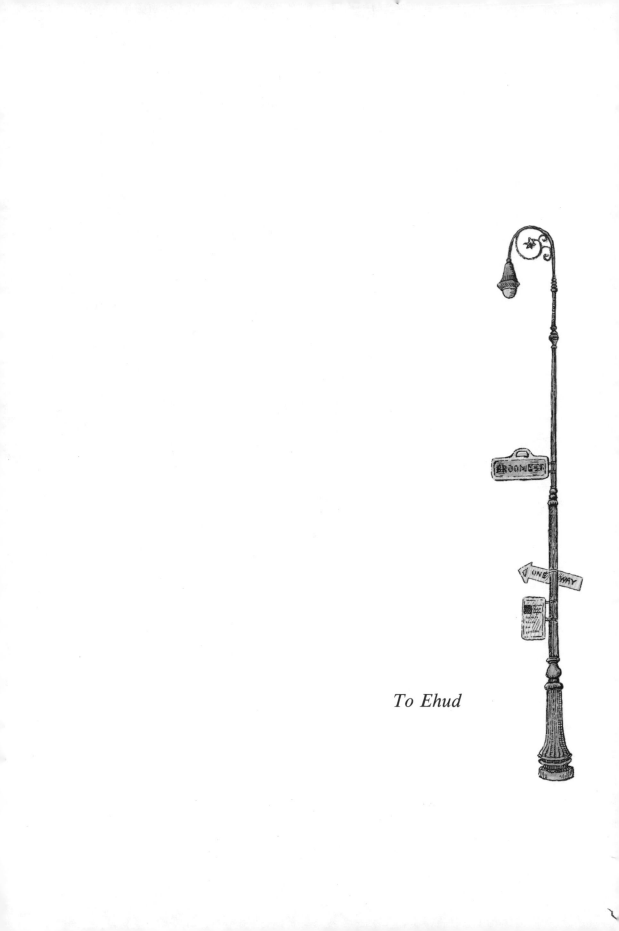

To Ehud

One Monday morning

the king,

the queen, and the little prince came to visit me.

But I wasn't home.

So the little prince said,
"In that case we shall return on Tuesday."

On Tuesday morning the king, the queen, the little prince,

and the knight came to visit me.

But I wasn't home.

So the little prince said,
"In that case we shall return on Wednesday."

On Wednesday morning
the king,
the queen,
the little prince,
the knight,
and a royal guard
came to visit me.

But I wasn't home.

So the little prince said,
"In that case we shall return on Thursday."

On Thursday morning
the king, the queen,
the little prince,
the knight, a royal guard,
and the royal cook
came to visit me.

But I wasn't home.

So the little prince said,
"In that case we shall return on Friday."

On Friday morning
the king, the queen,
the little prince,
the knight, the royal guard,
the royal cook,
and the royal barber
came to visit me

But I wasn't home.

So the little prince said,
"In that case we shall return on Saturday."

On Saturday morning
the king, the queen,
the little prince,
the knight, a royal guard,
the royal cook,
the royal barber,
and the royal jester
came to visit me.

But I wasn't home.

So the little prince said,
"In that case we shall return on Sunday."

6
FLOOR

On Sunday morning the king, the queen,
the little prince, the knight, a royal guard,

the royal cook,
the royal barber,
the royal jester,
and a little dog
came to visit me.

And I was home.
So the little prince said,
"We just dropped in to say hello."